WESLEY GAINES SCHOOL: K - 8
7340 E. JACKSON ST.
PARAMOUNT, CA 90723
(562) 602-6962

A GIFT FOR AMPATO

A GIFT FOR
AMPATO

SUSAN
VANDE GRIEK

WITH ILLUSTRATIONS BY

Mary Jane Gerber

A GROUNDWOOD BOOK
DOUGLAS & McINTYRE
VANCOUVER TORONTO BUFFALO

With special thanks to Dr. John Topic, Department of
Anthropology, Trent University, Peterborough, Ontario.

Text copyright © 1999 by Susan Vande Griek
Illustrations copyright © 1999 by Mary Jane Gerber

Groundwood Books/Douglas & McIntyre
585 Bloor Street West, Toronto, Ontario M6G 1K5

Distributed in the USA by Publishers Group West
1700 Fourth Street, Berkeley CA 94710

We acknowledge the financial support of the Canada Council for the
Arts, the Ontario Arts Council and the Government of Canada through
the Book Publishing Industry Development Program for our publishing
activities.

Canadian Cataloguing in Publication Data

Vande Griek, Susan, 1950-
A gift for Ampato

A Groundwood book.
ISBN 0-88899-358-7 (bound) ISBN 0-88899-359-5 (pbk.)

I. Child sacrifice — Peru — Juvenile fiction. 2. Incas — Juvenile fiction.
I. Gerber, Mary Jane. II. Title.
PS8593.A53855G53 1999   jC813'.54   C99-930264-7
PZ7.V2627Gi 1999

Printed and bound in Canada by Webcom Ltd.

To my parents

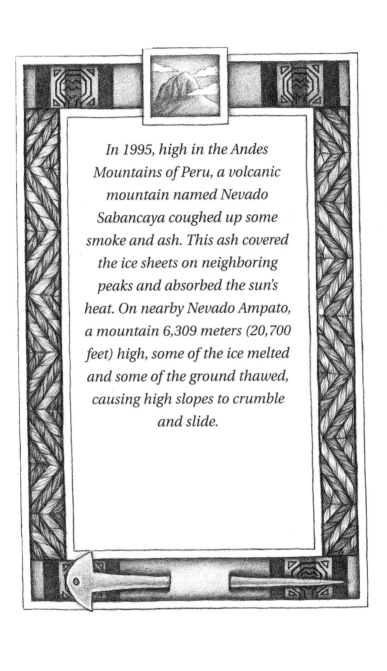

In 1995, high in the Andes Mountains of Peru, a volcanic mountain named Nevado Sabancaya coughed up some smoke and ash. This ash covered the ice sheets on neighboring peaks and absorbed the sun's heat. On nearby Nevado Ampato, a mountain 6,309 meters (20,700 feet) high, some of the ice melted and some of the ground thawed, causing high slopes to crumble and slide.

CHAPTER ONE

Riti pushed aside the heavy blanket and stepped outside the doorway. A light, cold rain stung her face. Grayness draped itself around the stone hut, the llama corral, the small fields. The mountain peaks had drawn the clouds about them, but at least today only rain was falling.

Riti raised her clever head to where she knew the gods were hiding. Her full lips spat out an oath and then she turned her back on Sabancaya, on Ampato. Her morning ritual completed, she withdrew back into her windowless hut and threw more dried llama dung on her small fire.

She took a handful of her precious store of corn from a cloth bag in the corner. She mixed the kernels with a few ashes and some water and set them to boil. Then she squatted down and waited. There was no rush to go outside in this weather. Besides, the dampness was making her hands and knees ache.

When the mote was done, she ate slowly. And when she had finished, she pulled her heavy brown shawl around her shoulders and her slightly graying head, picked up her pottery water jar, and went out to the llamas.

They were standing close together at the side of the corral. They immediately moved toward Riti when they saw her.

She greeted them quietly. "Ah, old one, young one, a wet day. So, never mind. Come now."

The old brown-and-white one and the young creamy white one followed her along a beaten path. They came to a spot where there was some fresh grass with very little ash covering.

"Stay," Riti said.

As the llamas began to graze, she walked on to her small plots of potato and quinoa plants. The plants were drooping and not just from dampness. The leaves were spotted and weighted down with wet ash. Riti clicked her tongue at the sight. They were growing so slowly. But then, she thought, why should the young things push their way into such a cold, gloomy world?

The mountain gods did not seem to be

in good moods lately. Doubtless the priests had made many offerings and said many prayers, but the apus seemed unmoved. It had happened before, Riti knew that.

Sometimes the apus withheld their life-giving water and the plants wilted and shriveled under the relentless gaze of Inti, the sun god. Once in a while they shouldered the rain clouds day after day, keeping the sun god's face hidden. And, on rare occasions, they roared and belched out smoke and ash, as they had just three days ago. Ever since then, the mountain gods had kept Inti and themselves covered with a blanket of the finest dust and ash.

Riti straightened up, for a moment not feeling the cold sting of the rain or seeing the drenched fields about her. Then she shook her head, picked up her water jar, trudged to the small stream to fill it, and carried it back to where the llamas were eating.

The young one raised her head from the grass and Riti rubbed her face in the long, shaggy neck. The old one continued to graze. At Riti's push, she lifted her head, gave a little spit, and reluctantly placed her delicate feet on the path. They neared the hut where there were sparse patches of grass. Riti told the llamas to stay and nibble.

The steep, thatched roof of her house looked sodden, but inside was dry. Riti stirred the fire, then pulled off her wet shawl and placed it nearby. She poured a cup of chicha from a small jug, allowing herself this little indulgence on such a miserable day.

The fermented corn drink warmed her and eased her aches. She sat on a mat by the fire, drying the heavy skirt of her dress, while within her, thoughts and memories stirred and smoldered.

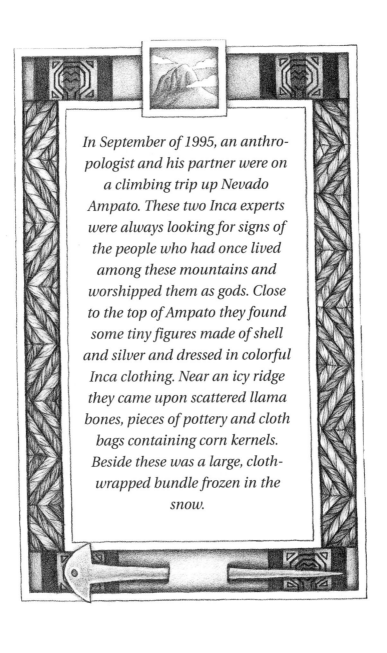

*In September of 1995, an anthro-
pologist and his partner were on
a climbing trip up Nevado
Ampato. These two Inca experts
were always looking for signs of
the people who had once lived
among these mountains and
worshipped them as gods. Close
to the top of Ampato they found
some tiny figures made of shell
and silver and dressed in colorful
Inca clothing. Near an icy ridge
they came upon scattered llama
bones, pieces of pottery and cloth
bags containing corn kernels.
Beside these was a large, cloth-
wrapped bundle frozen in the
snow.*

CHAPTER TWO

The he girls and women stood together in the gathering house. They were greeting the day from inside rather than out on the stone terrace, for gray cloud filled the valley and rain was falling. All their dark eyes faced in the direction where Inti usually appeared.

Obviously the mountain gods were not happy. Three days ago Sabancaya had rumbled and burped up smoke and ash. Since then, Ampato and the other peaks had hidden themselves, and the sun god.

For awhile all the girls had waited with sharp eyes and ears for more coughing and sputtering, but the apu of Sabancaya had been quiet.

Now Timta stifled a yawn and tried to keep her feet and hands from twitching as the prayers and praises went on, longer than yesterday, longer each day. For the mountains continued to hold around them the blankets of dust and ash, and today, rain as well.

Inti, sun god, please favor us.

Yes, Timta would not mind sitting on the terrace again, gathering some of Inti's warmth into her chilled bones.

Apu, god of Ampato, show us your face.

But sometimes the apus were frightening with their rumblings, their loud, flashing storms, or their thunderous slides of rock and soil, snow and ice. Still, Timta liked to look up and see the brown and green slopes of the mountains leaning against the sharp blue sky, their sturdy sides cradling her high valley.

Shuffling feet wakened her to the fact that the morning's praises were over. It was time for the first meal of the day.

Timta maneuvered her way over to Karwa. When the food was brought in from the cooking house, they sat together on a mat among the other girls and women. The pleasantly warm herb and corn mixture clung to their bowls and their empty stomachs.

"Karwa," Timta asked softly, "do you think all these extra prayers will do any good?"

Karwa, who knew much more about these things, nodded. "Oh, they must," she said. "Surely Inti and the apus will not ignore us, their children, for too long."

In her six full moons here with the acllas, Timta had never seen as many offerings as she had seen in the last three days. Even Karwa, who had been among the chosen girls for two full years, said the same. There had been ear after ear of corn, countless coca leaves, many small silver or shell llama figures. You would think, reasoned Timta, that the gods would be most pleased. But, though Sabancaya was quiet, the mountains still remained behind their clouds of dust, ash and rain, hiding themselves and the sun from the Inca.

Their bowls empty, Timta and Karwa joined the other girls in cleaning up. Then it was time for the day's work to begin.

They crossed the courtyard to the weaving house and stopped to watch one of the older women at her loom. She was making a beautiful piece of cloth.

The dark brown alpaca wool was woven tight and even. Rich red and yellow dyed threads formed a line of geometric figures along the edge.

"This will be for a priest's robe," said the woman, "worn for special ceremonies."

"So lovely," sighed Karwa. "Someday I hope to be able to do such fine work and to know all the designs passed down from our ancestors."

Timta also gazed in admiration, but with no such desire in her heart. The weaving required so much concentration, keeping the edges straight, the tension even, the patterns correct. She did not enjoy being strapped to her loom.

No, she much preferred the spinning,

taking the silky wads of llama or alpaca fleece in her hands and teasing out the unending, dense thread. At first it had been tricky, keeping the thread an even thickness. But now she had the knack, and as her fingers worked the wool and the yarn wound around the spindle, she could let her thoughts spin with it. That was what she especially liked.

Today, though, was another weaving session. Timta went to the loom she had left yesterday, sat on her mat, pulled the leather strap around her back and fastened it to the bar in front of her. Then she pulled against the warp threads that were wound between it and the bar pegged to the wall. Not liking the confined feeling, she picked up the weft thread reluctantly.

Timta glanced at Karwa, whose dark head was already intent over her loom, her long fingers moving swiftly, surely. Her friend, the one most like an older sister, was so hard-working, so full of goodness, so happy to be here.

Timta's own small fingers rested on the threads of her simple brown piece with the straight red border. Her thoughts went to home. Right now her grandmother was seeing to the house and the meals and her younger brothers, making sure they had their lessons in history and religion. Later, if it stopped raining, she would walk them through town to let them burn up some energy. Perhaps they would stop to watch the workers smoothing and fitting the stones for the newest state building.

Her father probably would be in one of the town storehouses at his post of quipu-camayoc. What would he be keeping count of today on his quipu, Timta won-

dered. Llamas, potatoes, sandals, soldiers? At home he had taught her how he did it. She had learned to tie a tiny knot on a brown quipu for every ten of their papas, a tiny knot on the yellow one for every ten ears of corn. She liked fingering the different colored strings, but she liked handling the potatoes or the corn cobs themselves much better.

The thought of hands reminded Timta that hers were idle at the moment, something the older women warned her to avoid. She leaned back against her strap and picked up the weft again. The women near her were talking as they worked, their fingers and their voices weaving in and out of Timta's sight and thoughts.

"Oh, such weather we're having and such a time, all that dust and ash."

"Not good, not good."

"We must see that the mountain gods are satisfied."

"And soon."

"Do you remember that other bad time, some five growing seasons ago?"

"Ah, yes, the dry spell. The apus sent no rain, no water for our papas."

"Yes, and there were all the offerings we made, llamas and young ones."

"Do you think it will be so again?"

"No doubt, no doubt."

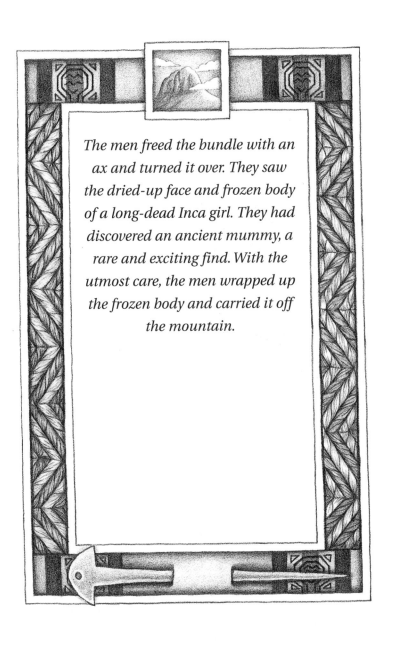

The men freed the bundle with an ax and turned it over. They saw the dried-up face and frozen body of a long-dead Inca girl. They had discovered an ancient mummy, a rare and exciting find. With the utmost care, the men wrapped up the frozen body and carried it off the mountain.

CHAPTER THREE

The next dawn was only dimly lit by a washed-out sun. The mountains were barely visible. One of the priests from the temple came to see the chosen women quite early in the morning.

He announced that a special ceremony was to be held that afternoon. The women and girls were to participate, and a young llama would be offered to the gods. This would encourage Inti and the apus to show themselves.

At once, all weaving was put aside.

Timta and Karwa followed the others to the gathering house to make ready for the ceremony. In came Mama, the chosen woman who was mainly responsible for the girls. She was everywhere, taking charge. She led them through the ritual prayers and praises, telling them what words to say, where and how to stand, what arm motions to use.

Timta tried hard to remember them all, but there were many. They practiced again and again. Some of the older girls beat out a rhythm on small skin drums to accompany the praises.

When Mama was satisfied that they knew their parts, she had the women bring from the wall niches the loveliest pottery bowls and the special golden ones. These the girls would fill with offerings for the gods. From large cloth bags brought in from the storehouses, they chose the largest, plumpest ears of corn, which spoke of a good harvest, and the finest coca leaves, which whispered of energy and contentment. A golden jar was filled with the best chicha, and golden cups were rubbed until they gleamed even in the dim light.

After everything was prepared, Mama said, "You have done well. I am pleased with how much you older girls have accomplished and with how far you younger ones have come in your learning. Now it is time to ready yourselves before we gather for the ceremony."

The girls hurried to the house in which they dressed and slept. Like the others, Timta wrapped and pinned around her the special dress she wore for ceremonies. She especially liked the bright red border along the bottom of the aksu. She took her chumpi and fastened it around her waist.

"Here, let me help you," said Karwa. She stepped behind Timta and deftly tied Timta's long, thick tail of hair to the colorful sash. Then Timta did the same for Karwa, though not as quickly or neatly, she thought.

Fingering the soft, thick wool of her red and yellow striped lliclla, Timta positioned it around her shoulders and clasped it together with her silver tupu. Hanging from the pin was a tiny cup on a thread. She touched it. It had been a present from her father when she had become one of the chosen. Karwa had one just like it, as well as a small, carved box and a little fox. All had been gifts from her family—one for being chosen and one for each year since.

The girls slipped on their best leather sandals and returned quickly to the gathering house. Mama calmed them as the ceremony was about to begin. She had them form a procession in the courtyard, the women in their bright llicllas carrying the golden bowls of offerings, the older girls with their small drums, Mama at the head holding the jar of chicha, and the younger girls at the end.

They wound their way out of the main gateway, stepping slowly across the square to the imposing temple. Someone had brushed the stones clean of ash, Timta noticed. The women took their places on the broad temple steps while the girls spread out across the bottom. A large, silent crowd had gathered before them. Probably most of the townspeople were there, so many faces that Timta could not focus on any of them.

The gray stone walls of the temple and other buildings lining the square blended into the hazy light of the day. Timta listened as the priests' assistants played on their quenas. The mournful music of the flutes hung in the air.

The priests came out of the temple and all the girls turned to look up. The reds, yellows and blues of their clothes and the gold jewelry that adorned their heads, necks and arms brightened the day. They shone, thought Timta, even if the sun did not.

Their deep voices filled her ears as they started their prayers. Then she and the other girls chanted their praises. One of the priests stepped forward and accepted a golden cup of chicha from Mama. He offered it up to Inti with pleas for him to overcome the darkness of the last few days.

Two priests took up the corn cobs and coca leaves. They spread some on the large ceremonial stone that sat on the temple terrace. The apus were asked to show no more displeasure, to clear away the clouds of dust and ash, to present themselves in all their glory so that their children might worship them properly.

Then the beating of a big drum began. The crowd grew tense. Out of the temple, the priests led a young llama, white as the mountains' snowy peaks. Red tassels bounced in its ears and on its halter as it stepped gingerly on its tiny hooves and turned its small, pointy head this way and that.

A gentle "oh" escaped from Timta's lips. She had never seen a llama so absolutely white.

She watched as it was led to the ceremonial stone. Though she had seen this offering ceremony before, she had never been so close, had never been a part of it. As the priests' prayers went on, her heart started pounding and her ears suddenly felt plugged. She glanced at Karwa, who was standing rapt and serious, her eyes on the llama. Timta looked back up just as the gold-handled knife moved with the priest's hand and slashed the llama's soft, young throat.

She stood still and open-mouthed as the llama's blood was collected in the priest's golden bowl. Spatters of red marked the now floppy, white neck.

The priest carried the bowl down the temple steps and stopped just in front of where Timta was standing. He implored Pachamama to keep their young plants and animals healthy until Inti and the apus again favored their people. He asked her to accept their very special offering. Then, in a slow stream, he emptied the bowl onto the earth mother.

At that moment the high gray cloud let slip a few bright rays of sun. The crowd, the women, the girls, raised their eyes to the sky. The priests and people gave a thankful yell. Only Timta's eyes remained fixed on the blood-soaked earth before her.

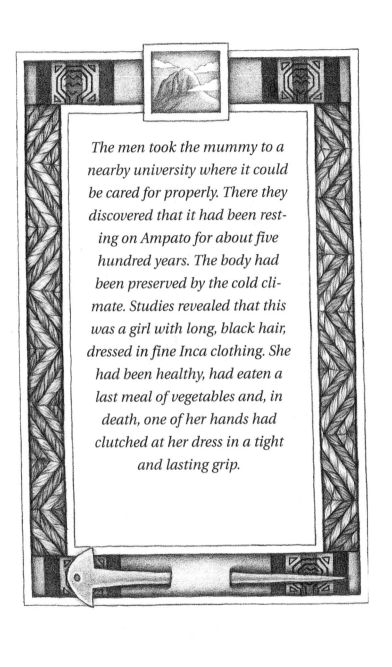

The men took the mummy to a nearby university where it could be cared for properly. There they discovered that it had been resting on Ampato for about five hundred years. The body had been preserved by the cold climate. Studies revealed that this was a girl with long, black hair, dressed in fine Inca clothing. She had been healthy, had eaten a last meal of vegetables and, in death, one of her hands had clutched at her dress in a tight and lasting grip.

CHAPTER FOUR

Timta did not sleep well that night. She was as restless as when she had first come to the acllas from her own home. In her dreams a silent condor had swooped down from the mountains, landed on the dead white llama and grasped the young body in its huge talons.

When the call came for greeting the day, Timta was already up and waiting. The girls and women assembled cheerfully, sure that yesterday's ceremony had done their world good. They reached the terrace only to be met by heavy bands of mist. Their spirits dampened. Still Mama led them in their ritual praises.

The morning meal was quiet. The girls finished quickly and went to the weaving house. Karwa was serious and frowning and did not offer any talk. Timta was troubled by thoughts of the llama, the blood sacrifice, her dreams.

No one's fingers flew this morning. Disappointment worked its way into the warp and weft on the looms and pulled with the straps against the girls' backs. Later, when it seemed to Timta that the drag of the day could no longer be endured, Mama entered the room.

"Chosen ones," she said to them, "we have special visitors."

Two of the priests entered behind her. They were not dressed as finely or colorfully as yesterday. Still, the girls were arrested by their appearance. The priests had visited before, of course, usually to check on some weaving or on some ceremonial matter. But it was rare. Today they made their way slowly around the room, ignoring the women but stopping by looms and speaking to the girls.

Timta thought they must be looking for the finest weaving, and as the priests drew nearer to her loom she began to feel embarrassed. They had paused by Karwa. Timta could not hear what they were saying, but she thought they were paying more attention to Karwa than to her cloth.

Then they were beside her. Timta felt a lump in her throat as they studied her face, laid their hands on her shining, dark hair, and asked her name. She murmured it.

"Ah, yes," one said. "I remember. You are daughter of Quispe, the quipu-camayoc. You have not been among the chosen for long, have you?"

"Six…six full moons," Timta stammered.

"Ah, yes," they repeated, nodding. Then, seeming satisfied, they left.

Mama said, "Back to work, girls," as she followed the priests out of the house.

Timta again leaned over her weaving. The priests' visit had not lightened the weight that seemed to pull at her today. Some of the girls whispered among themselves, speculating on the purpose of the visit. The older women said nothing, just looked at each other knowingly.

Very soon, Mama returned, told them all to get their llicllas and to meet in the courtyard. From there they proceeded to the temple as they had the day before, but this time they took no golden bowls, no offerings, no drums. Only themselves.

The mist had thinned, yet the air was heavy, the day dull. The chosen women and girls stood solemnly on the great stone steps. In the square, some people were gathering, mostly men—public workers from the nearby buildings, nobles in their bright cloaks, a few commoners in town for the day.

Near the back of the small crowd, an older woman was standing by herself. She clutched her matted brown shawl tightly around her. Her small, piercing eyes focused only on the acllas waiting on the steps. She studied each one in turn. Which of them, she was wondering, would become weavers of fine cloth, which preparers of the ceremonies, and which would serve for some other purpose?

Karwa stood patiently, straight and serene. Timta was feeling restless, not wanting to remember yesterday in this spot, the llama, the blood, not wanting to look at the stained earth in front of her. Her eyes roamed over the faces in the crowd. Suddenly they stopped as she recognized her father. His eyes were set on her face and he smiled. Timta felt a surge of warmth and smiled back at him.

The priests came out onto the temple steps. They offered a prayer to Inti and asked why he was hiding his face again today. They prayed to the mountain gods and asked why they did not throw off the blankets of dust and cloud and reveal themselves to their people.

The people were silent and the priests now addressed them.

"The gods are not pleased. Our offerings and sacrifices have not been enough. Our crops must grow healthy, our llamas strong. We must make further offerings. We must persuade the gods to send us their favors."

The tallest of the priests stepped forward and said, "On the third daybreak from now, we will hold our special sacrificial ceremony. A chosen young woman will be honored. She will carry our pleas and our prayers to Inti and to the gods of Ampato and Sabancaya. She will take a place on Ampato, our special mountain, to remind the apus of our needs and to show them our greatest respect."

A second priest descended the temple steps. He stepped in front of Timta, placed his hand on her head for a moment, then took her by the arm and led her up to the temple terrace. He stopped by the ceremonial stone, lifted his head toward the mountains, and spoke.

"We ask you, apus, to find favor with our choice."

Timta's doe-like eyes looked at the priest, toward the mountains, then out at the crowd. All their eyes were staring at her, at her healthy young body, her warm, brown face. Confused, she sought her father's face. He gazed at her for a moment, not smiling now, and then he bowed his head.

Timta dropped hers as well and saw the rust-red stains on the carved stone by her feet. It struck her then. She was to take the place of the llama.

At the back of the crowd, the lone, older

woman stared long and hard. The priest's announcement, the scene on the steps, and the girl with her llama-like neck, river of hair and tender face, all called up memories of another girl who had stood just so.

The woman's hand swiped at her eyes. As the girls and priests left the temple steps, she turned to face cloud-draped Ampato. She muttered aloud her dark thoughts. A few people near her frowned. She was jostled by the crowd as it broke up, but she pushed through the streets and the town, across the bridge to the slopes and up the empty, winding paths to her hut and her llamas.

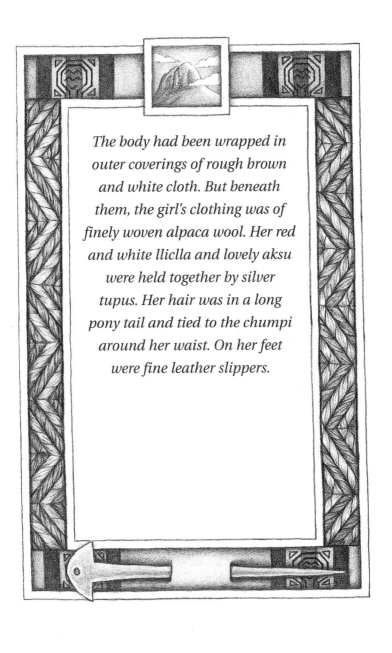

The body had been wrapped in outer coverings of rough brown and white cloth. But beneath them, the girl's clothing was of finely woven alpaca wool. Her red and white lliclla and lovely aksu were held together by silver tupus. Her hair was in a long pony tail and tied to the chumpi around her waist. On her feet were fine leather slippers.

CHAPTER FIVE

Timta left the temple steps in the company of Mama, who had to lead her away by the arm. The other girls stared and followed. They went back to their courtyard where they whispered among themselves. But Mama immediately set them to work preparing for the last meal of the day.

Some went to the cooking house where a stew was boiled and stirred. As the bowls were brought to the gathering house, the girls filled the large room with their anticipation and talk of the coming ceremony. Timta only sat, her imagination jumping with each new thought or fact her ears picked out of their conversations.

All of them congratulated Timta on the great honor she had been given. They brought bowls of food to her. They did not ask her to lift a finger. She wanted to smile at the kindness of the girls, but she felt unable to raise the corners of her mouth.

Timta was relieved when Karwa finally came to sit beside her, but she could not speak to her, the papas and corn catching in her throat.

Karwa touched Timta's arm. "It is overwhelming, isn't it?" she whispered.

Timta grabbed her friend's hand and held it tightly for a moment. Then she concentrated on getting through the evening meal. She was excused from the cleaning up. "No more of that for one such as you," the women said.

Mama told her that she was to go to rest early, for there were two very busy days ahead of them. So Timta went to the girls' house, unrolled her sleeping mat, spread out her blankets and lay down. As the day darkened, her mind played over its events, then imagined the ones to come.

Suddenly she had become the most special one, the chosen one among the chosen. Why her? She had been here just a short time. She certainly was not the most accomplished of the girls, still learning to weave, still learning the ceremonies and the preparations. And, she thought, watching Karwa, who was now walking across the room, she definitely was not the kindest or most devoted.

She closed her eyes and a few tears squeezed out.

Karwa pulled her mat close to Timta's. "Mama released me early so that I might keep you company. Oh, Timta, such a great honor you are chosen for. You are to carry our prayers, our pleas, to the gods themselves, to live with them on Ampato in glory for ever!"

More tears escaped from Timta's eyes. Karwa noticed them.

"Timta, what is wrong? Are you crying in your great happiness?" she asked.

"Oh, Karwa, I don't know. I am scared, I think."

"Ah," said Karwa, "it is only right to be a little scared. All the ceremonies and all the attention, wondering if you will do well. I would be nervous, too."

"No," cried Timta, "no, you wouldn't."

Karwa stroked Timta's hair gently. "It will be fine," she murmured. "All of us will help you. You are young and new to this, but I will stay by your side as much as I can. Oh, Timta, the gods cannot help but be pleased with you. Now try to ease your mind and sleep, special one."

But Timta lay there under her wool blanket for a long time, while images played behind her closed eyes. Finally, when the thinking had exhausted her, she fell into a short but deep sleep.

◆

She rose, dull and sluggish, like the morning sun. On the terrace, the cool air woke her slightly, yet, as the greetings of the day were chanted, she could not get her tongue to work.

The other girls talked easily through the morning meal. The sun, though weak and watery, riding in the gray sky, was at least visible. This seemed to have lifted almost everyone's spirits.

The weaving house was bustling, too, but Mama told Timta that she was not to work at her loom. Instead today she would be fitted for her special ceremonial clothes. Moving among the looms, they stopped by a woman who was just finishing a beautiful piece of alpaca cloth. It was creamy white with a very wide and rich red border. Woven within this was a fine pattern. Mama decided that it would be made into the lliclla.

They went on to one of the small storehouses across the courtyard. Here, from a supply of finished clothing, Mama chose a soft and lovely aksu. Though it was a bit too large for Timta, a multi-colored chumpi pulled it in nicely around her waist. Mama said there would be plenty of growing room in it for her in the afterlife.

Mama also chose two large pieces of llama wool and set them aside for wrapping cloths. Timta's feet were measured so that a pair of slippers could be made from pieces of soft llama skin. And finally, a headdress had to be prepared. Mama chose the red and brown feathers. One of the woman measured Timta's head and then set to work on it.

For most of the day Timta trailed behind Mama like a pet llama. She was very quiet. When all the clothing arrangements had been made, Mama, feeling a little concerned, took Timta to the gathering house. She fetched her a small cup of chicha, for this special occasion only, she said, and sat her down for a talk.

"Timta," she began, "you understand that this, for which you have been chosen, is the greatest honor any of us could receive."

Head down Timta nodded, almost wishing that she could speak freely. But she knew that this Mama was not as hers had been. Hers had listened to Timta's words eagerly as Timta had chatted about anything, everything.

No, this Mama was more like Timta's grandmother. She would teach and explain and tell you how everything must be a certain way, and she would be kind. But she was like the mountain peak you looked up to but did not get close to.

"You are young and have not been among us long," continued Mama. "Maybe you have been chosen for that very reason. You are perfect and pure, in body, heart and mind. The apus will be pleased. Now you must bear yourself with the greatest dignity and assurance. You are to go to a life among the gods, and it will be glorious."

Timta swallowed and looked up into Mama's firm face.

"That's right," Mama said. "Raise your head up. Carry your back straight. You are the chosen one among the chosen, and the next two days will be yours. You must let your grace and your reverence for Inti and the apus guide you, lift you up, so that you can see truly the wondrous thing that has happened to you. Now sip your drink and then go and rest for a little. Later you will be needed. I must check on the lliclla and the headdress."

When she was gone, Timta's trembling hands gripped the cup. She gulped down the corn drink. Then, not knowing what else to do, she did as Mama said and went to lie on her mat.

But she could not stay there. She got up and paced the cool, stone floor like a young viscacha caught in a trap.

Only when Karwa stood in the doorway did she stop. "Come," Karwa called, smiling and motioning. "You have a visitor. Your father is here."

Timta's heart kicked in hope. She hurried to the gathering house. Her father stood and raised his hands—those hands that every day counted up numbers of papas, llamas and people in their mountain region—and he placed them on the shoulders of his one and only daughter.

"We are so proud, so proud," he said excitedly. "You have brought the greatest honor to our family. When your mother died, I did not know what I would do, how

things would turn out. But when you were able to join the chosen and come here, I knew a place had been found for you. And now, well, a place even more special has been found."

He patted her dark head. "At the moment of your birth, the mountain gods sent down their first breath of spring. I knew then that you were special to them. And now, you will go to join them."

"Father," Timta began, but looking up into his smiling face and realizing she could no longer bury hers in his soft tunic as she used to, she could say no more.

"Grandmother and the boys send their blessings. They will see you at the ceremony. It will be the most special of days for us all."

Some of the older women were coming into the house, and all the buts stuck in

Timta's mind, never reaching her tongue.

"Now," her father said, "you will make us proud, as you have always done." He reached out to her, not seeming to know where to place his hand. Finally he touched her cheek for a moment. Then he turned to leave.

Timta could not watch him go. She did not see the sinking head, the drop of his shoulders, as he walked away.

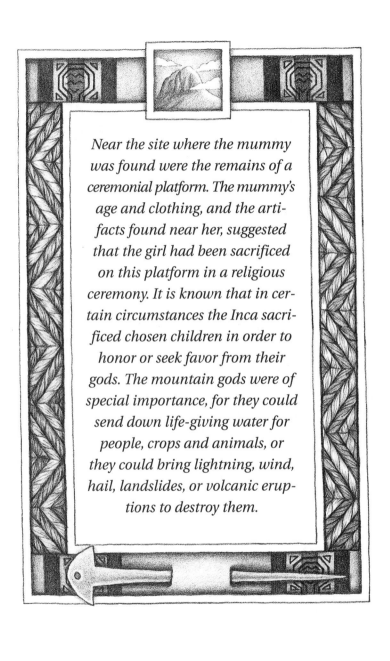

Near the site where the mummy was found were the remains of a ceremonial platform. The mummy's age and clothing, and the artifacts found near her, suggested that the girl had been sacrificed on this platform in a religious ceremony. It is known that in certain circumstances the Inca sacrificed chosen children in order to honor or seek favor from their gods. The mountain gods were of special importance, for they could send down life-giving water for people, crops and animals, or they could bring lightning, wind, hail, landslides, or volcanic eruptions to destroy them.

CHAPTER SIX

Riti spent most of the day working in her small field. Though she usually enjoyed this, she did not today. The earth was soggy, sticking to her hands. The potato and quinoa plants were gray and bedraggled, the wet ash clinging to their leaves. She gently worked her fingers over them, trying to clean them off, but it was slow, messy, and only somewhat successful.

The teasing sun lay behind a thin skin of cloud, doing little to dry things up.

Feeling discouraged and bedraggled herself, Riti finally returned to her hut. She stopped to see the llamas, talking and nuzzling with them for some time. Then she went to stir a fire.

She cleaned herself up as best she could and rubbed some of her moss powder into the chapped, sore skin of her hands.

Hungry, she brought out some chuño to boil for her meal. The dehydrated potatoes were getting a bit soft after months in storage. She ground up some and mixed them with a few beans and herbs in a stew, wondering if there would be many new ones to replace them.

If not, she was sure her neighbors in the village below would provide some from their storehouses, just as they now supplied her with corn and a few other necessities. The community had accepted her when she had simply shown up, alone, a widow. They had given her the llamas, first the old one, then later the young one. They had helped her build her hut up here where she wanted to be and, in exchange for the shelter, she tended their llamas when they brought them up to graze the high slopes.

The chuño was cooked and Riti ate, stopping often to think of all she had seen and heard in the town. She wondered again why she had been so restless yesterday, unable to work, why she had felt driven to go and walk the streets she used to walk and see the house she used to live in. This was something she never did now.

And then she had ended up near the temple and she had seen the girls, the girls of eleven or twelve summers, the healthy young girls with their innocent bronze faces and their dark, shining eyes and hair.

It had been too much like the other time, five years before, when the gods had withheld their water and extra offerings had been needed. Then the chosen had stood before the temple and one had been singled out. She, like the one yesterday, had been led up the steps, her body stiff, a bewildered look on her face.

Riti banged her bowl down and cradled her head in her hands as pain again swept through the arms that had held that one, the belly that had carried her, the eyes that had gazed lovingly upon her.

Oh, she had tried to feel honored, to feel the rightness, the necessity of the offering. She had tried to believe that, in such bad times, each of them must do the most for their gods, their people.

But what good had come of it? Still the plants had withered up, the dry spell had continued. The papas had been small and few, the corn cobs tiny. The apus had been given the most precious of gifts and they had given nothing in return. Worst of all, thought Riti, maybe they had not even noticed.

She raised herself, went to the doorway of the hut and pulled the blanket aside. At least, living here with her llamas, she no longer had to listen to the town's talk of her great honor, and, alone, she had found some escape.

She stared out at the night. An almost full moon had taken the sun's place behind the clouds.

The thoughts and feelings moving in her mind and heart traveled out across the terraced field, down the steep paths and into the high valley, through the streets of the town to that special building near the temple and the chosen girl who waited there.

◆

Timta sat up on her mat, her breath coming fast and shallow. A dream had woken her, a dream in which she had been walking, walking always upward, growing dizzy, finding it harder and harder to breathe.

She got up and stepped quickly until she reached the courtyard and the fresh air. The night was still and cool. There was some faint light from a shadowy moon. Timta took in deep gulps of air and tried to calm her rapidly beating heart.

Why me? The thought hammered again in her head. She was too young and knew too little to be picked for such an honor. She did not fit among the priests and the sacred, in the high world of the mountain gods. She only wanted to be out in the town among the other girls or at home working and playing with her family.

Truthfully, she had not wanted to come here. She had not wanted to be chosen by the priests and nobles to be one of the special women. So many girls thought it was the greatest thing. Not her.

But then, you were chosen, you did not get to choose. You went where you were told to go and did what your father, the priests and the nobles told you to do. If you were a woman you had to weave, to prepare food, care for children, maybe work in the fields. If you were a man you had to work for the great Inca or be one of his soldiers, or maybe work in the fields and on the roads and buildings.

Others, thought Timta, got to do the choosing. Not her. But she was not alone. She and her brothers did as their father or grandmother told them. Her father did as the nobles and administrators told him. The girls here obeyed the words of Mama and the older women. They listened to the priests, the priests to the oracles and the Inca himself, the Inca to Inti and the apus.

Timta sighed. This was all as it should be, wasn't it? Everything was taken care of, everyone was looked after. Oh, why was she having such strange thoughts?

She was weary, weary from sleeplessness, weary from thinking, weary from feeling.

Acceptance and honor—her father, Karwa and Mama had spoken of them.

Why did she not feel them as strongly as they did?

Timta drew in one more deep breath of the heavy night air. She shivered, then went silently back to her mat and her unsettling dreams.

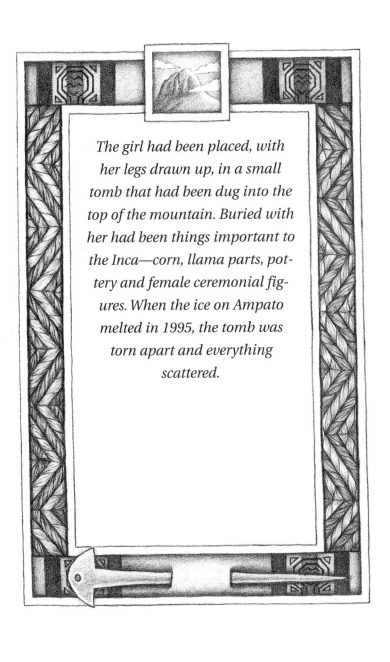

The girl had been placed, with her legs drawn up, in a small tomb that had been dug into the top of the mountain. Buried with her had been things important to the Inca—corn, llama parts, pottery and female ceremonial figures. When the ice on Ampato melted in 1995, the tomb was torn apart and everything scattered.

CHAPTER SEVEN

The mountain people woke to a day wrapped in a shroud of clouds, for at dawn Sabancaya had coughed up some more ash. The chosen women rushed the girls through their early rituals and meal. Then they kept them in the gathering house to make ready for the next day's ceremony.

Again corn, potatoes and coca leaves were sifted through and chosen to fill the special bowls. Small prayer bundles of corn kernels, coca leaves and llama fat were made up for the priests to leave at the sacred places they would pass on their way toward and up Ampato.

The girls dressed tiny figures of gold, silver or shell in small aksus, llicllas and red-feathered headdresses. These also would be left by the priests as offerings.

Under the direction of Mama, the music, songs, prayers and dance steps were practiced. She told the girls what they would be expected to do. She took extra time to show Timta her role. She demonstrated how and where she would stand on the temple steps when she was being honored, told her how she would be carried from the temple and through the town in a splendid litter on the shoulders of the priests' assistants.

The priests, dressed in their brightest clothes and adorned with their gold jewelry, would follow. And the people, in a swirl of color, would dance and sing to their departure. Then Timta, the priests, their assistants and llamas would begin the two-day trek up Ampato. The camp and rest spots had already been prepared along the way.

At this Timta felt her eyes start to water. Mama took Timta's chin in her hand.

"You are nervous," she said. "It is rightly so, but all will be fine. You have listened well, learned much and are stronger than you know. The journey up the mountain will be taken slowly and there will be coca leaves to chew. They will help you. Do not worry. Put your thoughts in the mountains with the gods where they must rest from now on."

Mama called Karwa to them. "Take Timta to the bath now for cleansing and purification," she said. "One of the women will be waiting there for you."

Karwa nodded. She took Timta by the arm and led her to the sheltered corner of the terrace with its sunken, stone-lined bath. There the woman helped Timta undress and step down into the cool water, the pure mountain water sent down to them by the apus.

Timta squatted and shivered as the woman bent over her to rinse her long hair. When she was finished, the woman left Timta to soak and purify herself for a few moments. Karwa came to kneel nearby.

As her body adjusted to the water's temperature and the scented herbs surrounded her, thoughts and words welled up out of Timta.

"The girls say that on Ampato the air will not fill my body as it does here," she said.

"Ah," answered Karwa, "that is because the air is finer, rarer. It is the air of the gods. But you will live among them and soon it will seem natural to you. I wonder if I will ever have the honor of joining you there?"

Timta stared at Karwa. "You would go willingly, wouldn't you?" she asked.

"Why, of course," her friend responded. "To be chosen for this of all things, to be allowed to offer yourself so completely to your people and your gods. Oh, yes. I could desire no greater honor or higher purpose in life."

Timta's relaxed body suddenly crumpled with gasps and sobs. Karwa, speechless, stared at her young friend. Then she gasped.

"Timta, Timta, you do not feel that, do you? You are not just nervous, a little

scared. You are unaccepting. You do not feel the honor, the rightness of it here." She touched her head. "Or here." And she touched her chest.

Slapping the water, Timta half shouted, "No, no. I do not."

Then, as she mastered control of herself, she found the courage to speak her most dangerous thought. "It is not what I would choose."

"Choose?" repeated Karwa. "What do you mean? We do not choose. We are the chosen. Here I am thinking you are so honored, so special. I never imagined you did not feel the same. I never thought about this choosing. Oh, Timta, I am sorry."

The woman returned to help Timta out of the water, to dry her and help her dress for the special evening. Karwa left them and went to the terrace.

She stood for awhile staring out toward the shrouded peaks, trying to clear her clouded thoughts.

Later, when the preparations for the next day were complete, Mama sent all the girls to their house to quiet themselves before the special evening meal. Karwa and Timta drew close to talk.

"I know I should feel honored to be the chosen one," murmured Timta. "So why do my mind, my heart keep saying, 'This is not what I would choose.' I have been given no choice before, have not expected any. I have only done the things I was told to do."

"Yes, you were chosen to come here and so you did," said Karwa. "Still, I have felt sometimes that you were not really comfortable here. I thought it might just take you more time, but maybe it is not that. Maybe it is not a good place for you. Maybe you were not meant to be chosen. As for me, I have felt it was right ever since I arrived."

Timta rested her head on her palm. "I cannot see myself among the gods, Karwa. I only want to stay here among my people and the llamas in this stony valley, where I can smell papas cooking, bury my nose in my lliclla on cold days, or spend a morning feeling soft wool spinning out through my fingers. I like looking up to the mountain peaks, but I do not want to be up there among them. Oh, Karwa, you are so good, so believing, so sure of things," Timta uttered. "Why can't I be like that?"

Karwa paused, considering. Finally she said, "I think we are each as we are, Timta.

What is right for me maybe is not what is right for you, no matter what the priests or the women say. I would gladly go to the gods for my people, for you. To make such a sacrifice is what I long for. Can you see that, Timta? Do you understand? I would go for you."

Timta looked into the deep pools of Karwa's eyes and at her smooth, untroubled brow. Just then one of the women came to call the girls to their meal.

"We will talk later," whispered Karwa. "Listen. See if you can hide away some food while we are eating."

"Why?" asked Timta, but there was no time for an answer. The girls stood and smoothed their aksus and followed the woman quietly to the gathering house.

The meal was, indeed, a special one in Timta's and the gods' honor. Fresh fish had been carried by runners from the coast. Its pleasing odor filled the room. There were papas, fluffy quinoa mixed with beans and peppers, and tiny corn cakes, as well as a small cup of chicha for each of them.

But Timta did not really taste any of it. Nor could she figure out how to hide any of the food, especially with so many eyes constantly resting on her.

During some of the prayers and blessings, however, Karwa managed to stash away some papas and corn cakes, wrapping them in a small piece of cloth.

When the meal was finished at last, the girls and women went back to their houses to make sure their brightest llicllas and softest aksus were ready for the next day. The girls were to go to rest early so that they would be fresh for the morning's ceremony with the offerings at the temple, the procession through town and out of the valley, the singing and the dancing.

As they prepared for sleep, Karwa spoke quietly. "Have you understood me, Timta?" she asked. "I mean it when I say I will go for you."

"But…it would never be allowed," stammered Timta. "The priests, they would not…"

"Ah," interrupted Karwa, "this is one time the priests would not have first choice. But it means that you would have to leave our people, our high valley. In the morning you can be gone and I will offer myself in your place. At such a time they will surely accept me. I know Mama would urge them to do so. But tonight, Timta, you would have to follow a path of your own choosing. Will you?"

Timta could not answer. Her thoughts were turning round. She wanted to go, but what could she do if she did? She could not go home. She would have to leave the valley. Where would she go? Out to the fields, along the stone roads, up the mountain paths? No, not higher up the mountains, she thought, remembering her dream.

Tahuantinsuyu was a large kingdom and she knew so little of it. She would be so alone. She had never been on her own.

And then there was her friend. How could she run off and let Karwa take her place?

Finally, as she unfolded her blanket, Timta spoke. "With all my heart I thank you for your offer, Karwa. But it is too much. You cannot sacrifice yourself for me."

"No," said Karwa, "I would not be. This, you see, is what I am here for. I know it. I burn with it in here." She placed a hand on her chest. "It is my path. Do you know yours, and do you have the strength to follow it?"

"I do not know," murmured Timta. "I do not know anything with the clearness that you do. I only know that my choice would not be the one laid out for me. My path would not be the one that leads up the mountain. But where would I go? And what if the priests' men or the soldiers came after me?"

"These things I do not know," Karwa answered. "Oh, Timta, you have made me see how blessed and fortunate I am. What others have chosen for me is what I would choose myself. For you, this is not so. Now you must decide. Will you allow others to choose or will you take that burden on yourself?"

Timta closed her eyes and swallowed hard. Then she looked into Karwa's face and managed to smile for the first time in two days.

"I will travel my own way," she stated.

Karwa smiled back. "I will help you," she replied. "Now quickly, dress warmly before we lie down to rest. Later, when all is quiet, you must leave."

Timta slipped her leather sandals and warm lliclla under her blanket. Then she and Karwa lay still and waited.

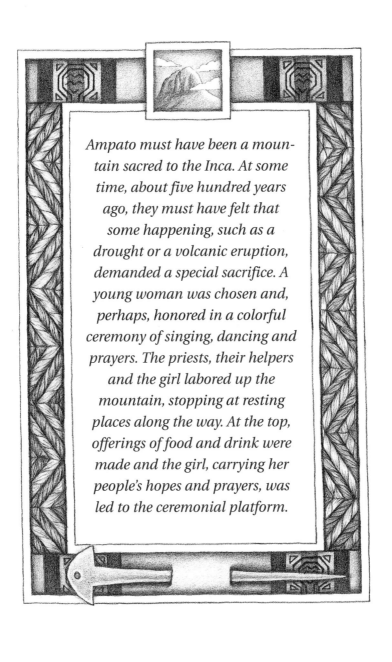

Ampato must have been a mountain sacred to the Inca. At some time, about five hundred years ago, they must have felt that some happening, such as a drought or a volcanic eruption, demanded a special sacrifice. A young woman was chosen and, perhaps, honored in a colorful ceremony of singing, dancing and prayers. The priests, their helpers and the girl labored up the mountain, stopping at resting places along the way. At the top, offerings of food and drink were made and the girl, carrying her people's hopes and prayers, was led to the ceremonial platform.

CHAPTER EIGHT

Rain or sun, the llamas brought light to Riti's day. On this dull one, she had spent time with them, cleaning up their coats a bit and finding them a new patch of grass to graze. She had been in the field as well, poking around among the gray and sun-starved potato plants.

Later, in her hut, she ate her chuño and sat by the fire. She was tired tonight. All day her mind had been busy digging up memories, turning them over, spreading them out before her. The memories would not dry up or wither away. Her heart's cries kept them fresh.

She took out a bag of the fleece that she and the villagers had sheared from the llamas. She began to work over it, teasing some of the clumps and separating the fibers. The soft, oily wool felt good against her sore fingers. Working with it usually relaxed her. But not tonight.

Finally she gave it up and went to lie on her mat. She pulled the blanket up around her face. The woven wool from old one and young one usually comforted her. But not tonight.

She thought of tomorrow, the day of the special ceremony at the temple in the valley. She would not go. She would not watch and sing and chant as she had done once before while the chosen one was carried above the people, their pleas nesting among the feathers of her headdress.

The face of the chosen girl on the steps the other day floated in Riti's mind. It became the face of the one who had gone before, her special one. And she, Riti, doing what honor demanded, had been unable to help her lost-looking child.

No, she would not watch it again. Not tomorrow, not ever. Nor did she want to watch the apus for their response.

She roughly pushed away her blanket, got up and paced the hut for a long time, her feet and her head knowing no quiet. When thinking was no longer bearable, she rolled up her sleeping mat, her blankets, her only other dress, and pulled on her heavy shawl, her old hat, her sandals. She took her bags of chuño, corn and beans, and her jar of chicha.

She carried the things to the corral,

then went back for her spindle and her bag of wool. The llamas came to her and she split her load between their backs. Then she put her hand on the old one's stately neck and told them both to come.

•

When the house had been silent for what seemed like hours, Timta sat up and pulled on her lliclla. Karwa stirred. She handed Timta the wrapped bundle of food from supper and helped her tie it to her chumpi. On tiptoe, with Timta carrying her sandals, the two stole from the room and made their way to the courtyard.

A large moon was hovering behind a thin wall of cloud. A cool, slight breeze was blowing.

"You must keep moving," whispered Karwa, "until you are well on your way.

Keep to the side streets in town and look out for the night watchmen. They are probably walking about. You know which road you will take?"

"Yes," Timta answered, putting her feet in her sandals. "I will cross the river and take the road down away from the mountains toward the coast."

The girls stood silent for a moment. Then Timta turned to her friend and said, "I cannot believe I am doing this. I will never forget you, Karwa. Never."

Karwa smiled. "Of course you won't. You will think of me whenever you look up to the mountains. That is where I will be."

Timta pressed into Karwa's hand the tiny cup on a string which she had untied from her own tupu. "Please, this is for you," she said. "You must add it to the one you have. Such generosity and goodness as yours could never be contained in just one."

Karwa hugged Timta to her. "Go, and remember, if you do not lose heart, you will not lose your way. Tomorrow, because of you, I will go where my heart leads." She turned away quickly and went inside.

Timta looked after her, then quietly passed through the gateway. She skirted the square and the stone temple that loomed dark and commanding in the half-light. She hurried from them, hugging the sides of houses, their cold stone and the night air making her tremble.

Soon she was outside the walls of her own home and courtyard. She gazed longingly at the doorway, wanting to be inside again with her father, her brothers, her grandmother. And all of a sudden she thought of the great dishonor she would bring them when her disappearance was discovered. She pressed her hands and face against the smooth stones and moaned. But still she could not enter. For whether she left or stayed, she knew that by tomorrow she would be gone from them forever.

Slowly Timta straightened up and continued past. She saw no one.

At last she came to the end of a small street that opened out onto a wider one. This, she could see, led onto the keshwa chaca that crossed the river. The suspension bridge was swaying gently with the breeze. On the other side was the road that soon wound down out of sight of the town.

Timta stepped out on the broad street, eager to cross the bridge.

At that moment, two of the town's

guards walked near on patrol. They saw her before she saw them. They stopped in front of her.

Timta drew up, caught unawares.

"Well," said one of the guards. "Who are you, child? What are you up to, out so late?"

"I…I am Timta," she answered truthfully, knowing that now she would have to think faster than she'd ever had to before.

"And you are doing what, going where?"

"I was in town for the day, with my family," Timta said. "We came to make special offerings. But there were such crowds, so many people getting ready for tomorrow's ceremony. We got separated. I looked and looked for them, with no luck. I was so tired. I did so much walking. And then I sat down near the temple and fell asleep. I only just woke."

The guards laughed.

"Please," whispered Timta, "I need to go home, to find my family. They must have given up searching for me for today. They must have left the town and gone back to our village to wait for me. Please, let me go, just over there, on the other side of the river."

"Ah," said the second guard, now standing beside her. "I see. Yes. Look over there." And he pointed across the chaca.

The first guard turned. Timta peered past him. On the other side of the river she could make out a figure standing quite still between two llamas.

"Yes, yes," she breathed in unexpected relief. "There they are, my father and the llamas. They have waited for me across the river, waited for me to find my way to the bridge."

"Well," said the guard, "you must hurry up then. It grows very late. Keep them waiting no longer. You are lucky we have some moonlight tonight." He stepped aside. "Careful on the bridge now."

Timta ran past him onto the swaying chaca and tightly grabbed the grass-rope cable. She moved quickly across and stepped onto the road. With her heart thumping, she hurried up to the figure standing there with the llamas. She saw now that this was a woman under the hat and cloaked in the heavy shawl.

"Please," Timta murmured again. "The guards, they think you are waiting for me. Please, may I go with you, just for a little way."

Riti looked down into the young, hopeful face, the face she had seen on the temple steps and in her troubled dreams.

"You may journey with me," she said. "I am leaving the valley and these mountains, finding my way as I go. Does that suit you?"

Timta nodded.

Both of them turned to look once more at Ampato, mostly hidden in cloud and darkness. One muttered an oath, the other uttered a blessing.

Then, with the old one and young one, their feet feeling for the uneven stones, they started out on the steep, winding road.

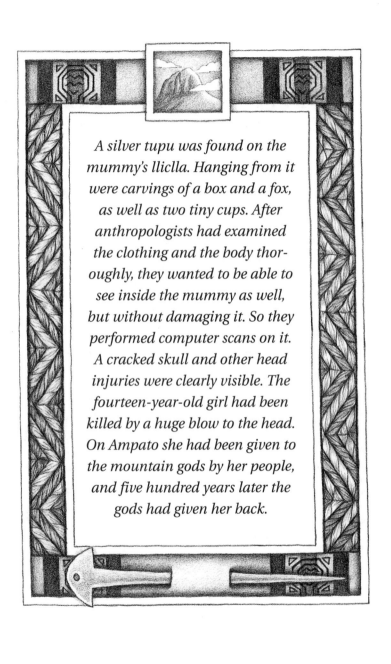

A silver tupu was found on the
mummy's lliclla. Hanging from it
were carvings of a box and a fox,
as well as two tiny cups. After
anthropologists had examined
the clothing and the body thor-
oughly, they wanted to be able to
see inside the mummy as well,
but without damaging it. So they
performed computer scans on it.
A cracked skull and other head
injuries were clearly visible. The
fourteen-year-old girl had been
killed by a huge blow to the head.
On Ampato she had been given to
the mountain gods by her people,
and five hundred years later the
gods had given her back.

AUTHOR'S NOTE

This novel is a mixture of fact and fiction. In *A Gift for Ampato*, the parts you have read about the mummy at the start of each chapter are true. The Ice Maiden, as she is called, was found on Nevado Ampato by Johan Reinhard and Miguel Zarate in September, 1995. Scientists and anthropologists continue to study the mummy in order to better understand the girl and her people.

The Inca of Peru established a large and complex empire in the 1400s and early 1500s. The things they made and the stories and traditions they passed down, as well as other people's historical records have given us a picture of their time. However, the Inca had no written language and so left no written records of their own lives. We do not know who the Ice Maiden was or exactly what circumstances or ceremonies brought her to Ampato.

The story of Timta, Riti and Karwa is made up. It is fiction. In writing about them, I have tried to be accurate in the everyday details of their lives, but some things are not known so I have used my imagination.

In the structured society of the Inca, community was very important. A person had definite responsibilities and very few choices. Riti probably would not have lived on her own and would not have thought of turning her back on the gods. Most likely, Timta would not have questioned her role and would not have thought of leaving her arranged place.

But as definite and limited as things might have been for the Inca, I like to imagine that someone, sometime, might have questioned what was normal, rebeled in some way, or dreamed of different possibilities.

GLOSSARY

acllas - girls who were chosen to serve the state and temple

aksu - a wrap-around dress that was fastened with tupus

alpaca - a llama-like animal with long wooly hair

apu - mountain god

chicha - a drink made from corn that has been boiled and fermented

chumpi - a woven sash worn around the waist

chuño - freeze-dried potatoes; the Inca would spread the potatoes on the ground, let them freeze, then thaw, then squeeze the juice out and keep them in storage

coca - a shrub whose leaves were chewed by the Inca

Inca - the people who established an empire in Peru before the Spanish conquest in the 1530s; their ruler was also called the Inca

Inti - the sun god

keshwa chaca - rope bridge; some Inca bridges were made by twisting and braiding heavy ropes out of grass and suspending them between rocks or stone posts

llama - an animal native to the Andes and related to the camel; the Inca used it as a pack animal and also for its wool, skin and meat

lliclla - a woven shawl that was fastened with a tupu

mote - a food made by boiling corn kernels with herbs or ashes

Pachamama - earth mother

papas - potatoes

quena - a small flute, often made of bone

quinoa - a grain grown in the Andes

quipu - a device of colored strings onto which the Inca tied knots in order to keep counts and records of things such as llamas, crops or people

quipucamayoc - the keeper of the quipu

Tahuantinsuyu - the four quarters of the world; the Inca word for their empire

tupu - a long straight pin used to fasten clothing

viscacha - a rodent with soft gray or brown fur, related to the chinchilla and living in the Andes

FURTHER READING

If you are interested in finding out more about the Ice Maiden and other Inca mummies, or about the Incas and Peru, you could look for the following:

The Inca, Indians of the Andes by Sonia Bleeker (Wm. Morrow, 1960)

Secret of the Andes by Ann Nolan Clark (Viking, 1952)

Peru, The Land and *Peru, The People* by Bobbie Kalman (Crabtree, 1994)

Discovering the Inca Ice Maiden, My Adventures on Ampato by Johan Reinhard (National Geographic Society, 1998)

National Geographic magazine articles:

"Lost Empire of the Incas" by Loren McIntyre (December, 1973)

"Sacred Peaks of the Andes" by Johan Reinhard (March, 1992)

"Peruvian Mummies" by Johan Reinhard (June, 1996)

"Sharp Eyes of Science Probe the Mummies of

Peru" by Johan Reinhard (January, 1997)

"Research Update: New Inca Mummies" by Johan Reinhard (July, 1998)